FOX RIVER GROVE PLD

P9-DCP-825

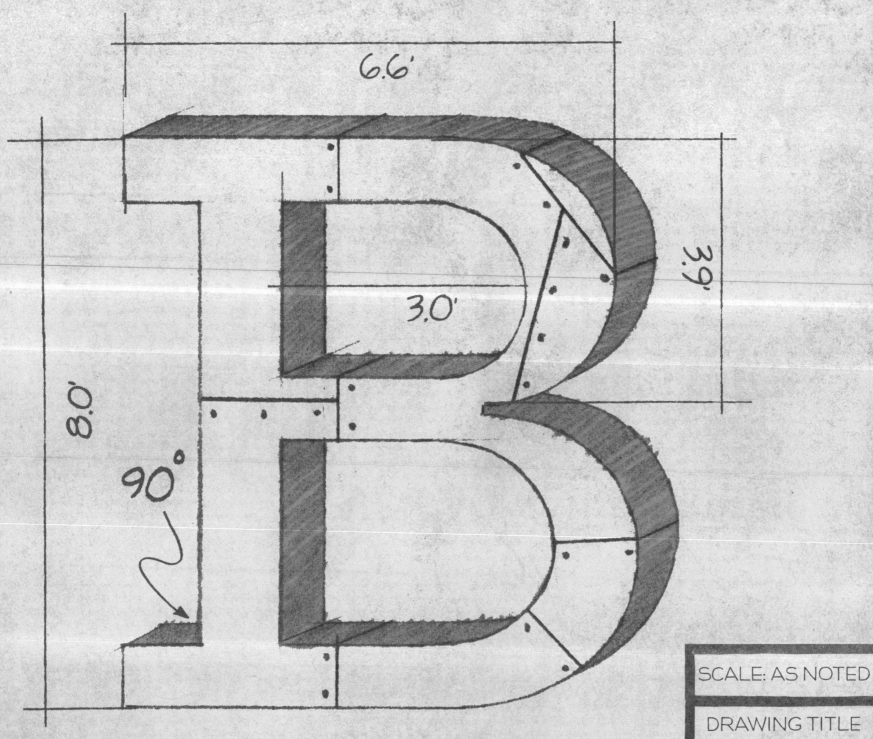

6.6'

3.9'

3.0'

8.0'

90°

SCALE: AS NOTED

DRAWING TITLE
LETTERS
A-B

A-2.1

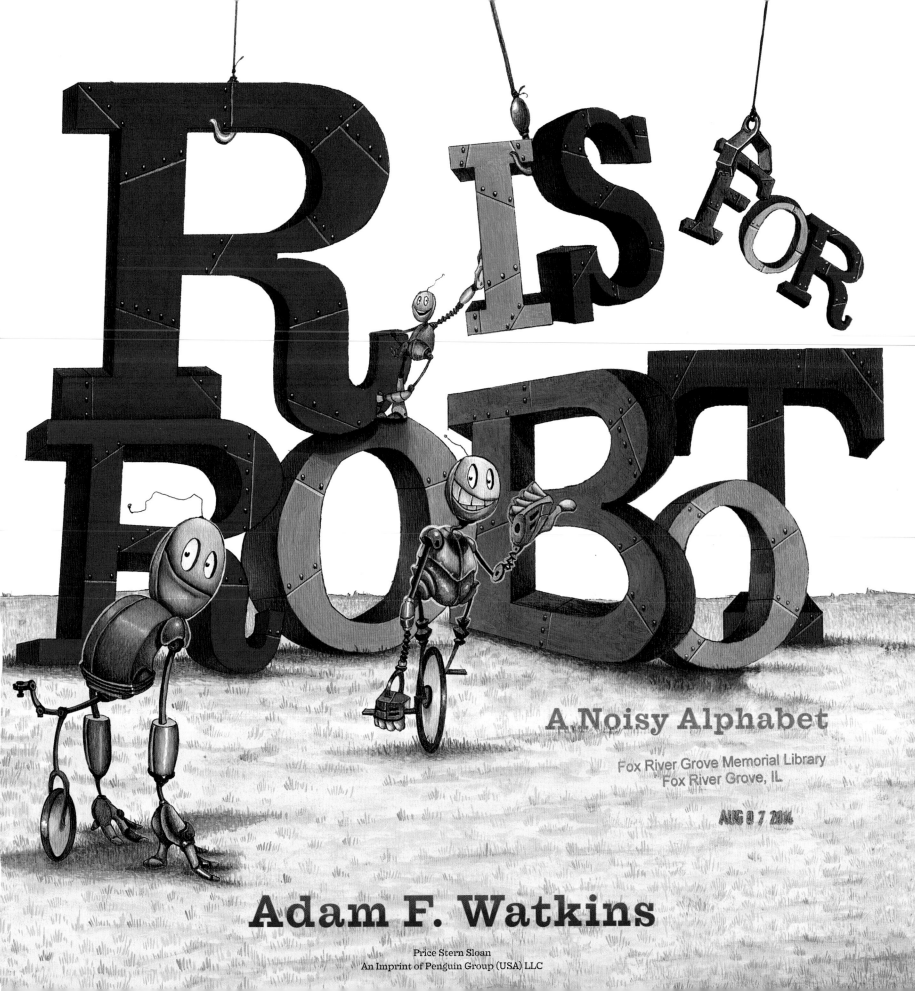

R IS FOR ROBOT

A Noisy Alphabet

Fox River Grove Memorial Library
Fox River Grove, IL

AUG 0 7 2014

Adam F. Watkins

Price Stern Sloan
An Imprint of Penguin Group (USA) LLC

For Rita and Scott

PRICE STERN SLOAN
Published by the Penguin Group
Penguin Group (USA) LLC, 375 Hudson Street, New York, New York 10014, USA

USA | Canada | UK | Ireland | Australia | New Zealand | India | South Africa | China

penguin.com
A Penguin Random House Company

Penguin supports copyright. Copyright fuels creativity, encourages diverse voices, promotes free speech, and creates a vibrant culture. Thank you for buying an authorized edition of this book and for complying with copyright laws by not reproducing, scanning, or distributing any part of it in any form without permission. You are supporting writers and allowing Penguin to continue to publish books for every reader.

The publisher does not have any control over and does not assume any responsibility for author or third-party websites or their content.

Copyright © 2014 by Adam F. Watkins. Published by Price Stern Sloan, a division of Penguin Young Readers Group, 345 Hudson Street, New York, New York 10014.
PSS! is a registered trademark of Penguin Group (USA) LLC.
Manufactured in China.

Design by Christina Quintero and Giuseppe Castellano
The art was created in pen and ink and oil paint on board.

Library of Congress Cataloging-in-Publication Data is available.

ISBN 978-0-8431-7237-9
1 3 5 7 9 10 8 6 4 2

drip
drop

FLICK

GRRRr

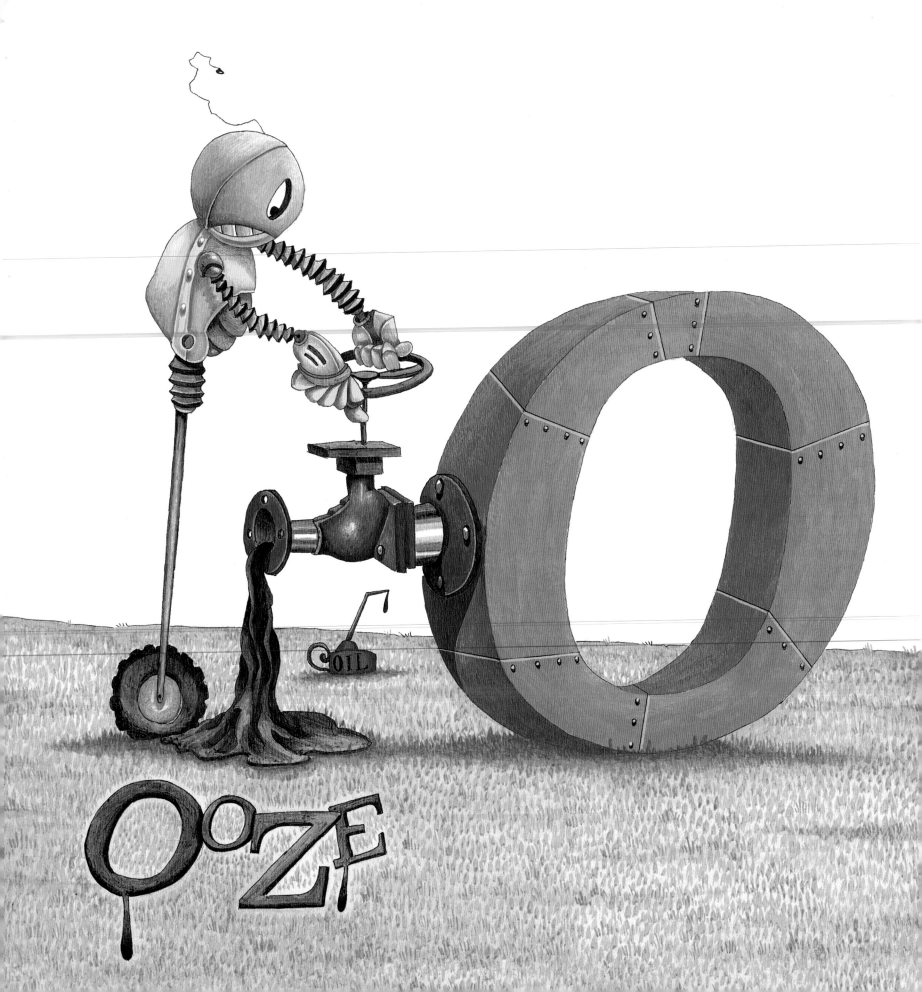

squeak